P9-CPV-900

# Sabrina

## The Teenage Witch™

# The Troll Bride

By Joseph Locke
"SABRINA, THE TEENAGE WITCH"
Based on Characters Appearing in Archie Comics
and the Television Show Created by Nell Scovell
Developed for Television by Jonathan Schmock
Based on the Episode Written by Nick Bakay and Frank Conniff

Simon Spotlight

Photographs by Don Cadette

 SIMON SPOTLIGHT

An imprint of Simon & Schuster Children's Publishing Division

1230 Avenue of the Americas

New York, New York 10020

™Archie Comic Publications Inc. © 1998 Viacom Productions Inc.

Image on page 10 © 1998 PhotoDisc, Inc.

All rights reserved including the right of reproduction in whole or in part in any form. SIMON SPOTLIGHT and colophon are registered trademarks of Simon & Schuster. Manufactured in the United States of America

First Edition          10 9 8 7 6 5 4 3 2

Library of Congress Catalog Card Number 97-62113

ISBN 0-689-81880-7

abrina frantically searched her bedroom for her biology notebook.

"Notes, notes, notes," she muttered breathlessly to herself.

Harvey's notes were a scribbly mess. That's why Sabrina and Harvey decided to use Sabrina's notes to study for their biology final. But now the notebook was lost!

Sabrina ran out of her room and found Salem in the hallway.

"Salem, have you seen my notebook?" she asked.

"Nope," the cat replied. "Why don't you just use a 'Finding' spell from your book of spells?"

"Great idea!" Sabrina exclaimed. She went back to her room and opened the magic book. When she found what she needed, she closed her eyes and said, "Finder of Lost Things, help me find my biology notes."

Sabrina then opened her eyes and looked around. But nothing had happened—her notes were still lost!

Suddenly there was a clap of thunder from the linen closet. A little bearded man in a velvety suit and top hat came bursting out. He headed straight for Sabrina's room.

"Ahh! Who are you?" Sabrina asked.

"I'm Roland, Finder of Lost Things!" he said.

Roland handed Sabrina a thick stack of papers. "Just sign this, please," he said. "It's the standard contract."

Eager to get her notes back, Sabrina signed the papers without reading them.

"Okay, stand back," Roland said. He raced around the room so fast, he was a blur. All of a sudden, he stopped and handed Sabrina her notebook.

"Wow!" Sabrina said. "Thanks!"

But Roland didn't leave. "Now, about my standard fee," he said.

"What's that?" Sabrina asked.

"Anything in this room," Roland replied. "It's in the contract you signed." He inspected Sabrina's clock radio, bed, everything on her shelves. Then he turned to her and grinned. "I'll take *you*!" he said.

"*Me*?" Sabrina blurted.

Roland nodded. "Yes, I want your hand in marriage!"

Marriage?! Sabrina had to escape! Grabbing her school books, she ran from her room, down the stairs, and past her surprised-looking aunts.

"I-don't-have-time-to-deal-with-him-but-there's-a-troll-in-my-room-and-I'll-tell-you-about-it-later!" she said to them. Then she was gone.

Hilda and Zelda looked at each other.

"Did she say 'troll'?" Zelda finally asked.

But Sabrina did not escape Roland as she'd hoped. He followed her to school and caused nothing but trouble.

The pesky troll disrupted her biology class and got into a loud argument with Mr. Pool. At lunch he jumped on a table and tried to pick a fight with Harvey. Roland kept calling Harvey "Farm Boy." Harvey didn't like that at all.

When Harvey asked her who Roland was, Sabrina said, "It's a funny story. I'll tell you later." What *could* she say? Sabrina just hoped she could make it through the day without getting into any *real* trouble!

When school was finally over, Sabrina took Roland home.

"She *did* say 'troll'!" Zelda said when she and Hilda saw Roland.

"What's he doing here?" Hilda asked.

Sabrina told them the whole story. They decided Sabrina needed a good lawyer who specialized in troll law. After searching the Purple Pages, they found Stuart Clarkson.

When Mr. Clarkson appeared, the aunts showed him the contract Sabrina had signed.

"It's hopeless," Mr. Clarkson said, shaking his head.

"What?" Sabrina exclaimed. "I'm *not* getting married!"

He looked up from the contract. "According to this contract, you are," he said grimly.

Frustrated, Sabrina went into the living room. Roland was asleep on the sofa. "Look, Roland," she said, waking him up. "There is no *way* I'm marrying you."

"I'm sorry," Roland said sarcastically. "I didn't hear that."

"I'm *not* marrying you!" Sabrina went on. "I'm flattered you chose me over a clock radio, but this is *not* my idea of a romance!"

"And Farm Boy *is?*" Roland asked.

"Yes, he is," said Sabrina. "And stop calling him that!"

Roland stared at her for a moment, then got up and shuffled sadly up the stairs.

Sabrina followed him. "Look," she said, "you still deserve a fee for finding my notes. Sure you don't want that clock radio?"

"No," the troll said. "I've found a lot of things, but I guess I'm still looking for love." Then he went into the linen closet and disappeared in a flash of light.

Salem was curled up on the hamper, watching. "What did you do to him?" he asked.

"Nothing," Sabrina said, "I just—" She stopped as she spotted Roland's hat. "He left his hat!" she said. "I'll be right back. I'm going to take it to him."

Sabrina stepped into the linen closet with Roland's hat. An instant later, she was outside his castle. It was a troll-sized castle. The front gate was open, and Sabrina walked into the courtyard.

She went up to a small door and knocked once, then again. No one answered. Sabrina didn't even hear any sounds inside. She cautiously turned the handle and pushed open the door.

"Hello, Roland?" she called.

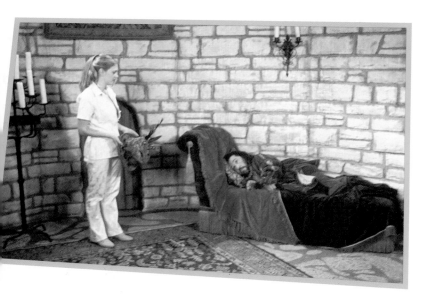

Roland was lying on a sofa. "What do *you* want?" he asked, not bothering to look at her.

"You left your hat," Sabrina said as she closed the castle door. "I'm sorry things didn't work out as you planned." There was no response from the troll.

"Well, I've got to go study," Sabrina finally said. But when she turned to leave, the door wouldn't open! "The door's stuck," she said.

Roland jumped to his feet, grinning. "It's not stuck, it's locked! You're trapped here forever, Sabrina! Remember, I'm a *finder,* not a *loser!*" He clapped his tiny hands together and laughed a cold, victorious laugh.

"Oh, no!" Sabrina cried, turning away from Roland. She shook the door handle desperately.

"So, when should we have the wedding?" Roland asked.

*"Never!"* Sabrina shouted.

Ignoring her comment, Roland said, "I think June would be better."

Sabrina gave up. "You can't keep me here, you know," she said with a sigh.

"Yes, I can!" Roland laughed again. "You signed a contract, remember? A legally *binding* contract!"

Meanwhile back at Sabrina's house, Mr. Clarkson was still paging through his stack of thick law books.

Salem hopped up onto the table and announced, "Uh, Sabrina went to return Roland's hat an hour ago and hasn't returned."

"Oh, no!" Zelda cried. "*That* old troll trick!"

"And it's perfectly legal," Mr. Clarkson said.

The aunts hurried to the linen closet. A moment later, they knocked on the door of Roland's castle. The aunts assured Sabrina that a good lawyer was working hard on getting her out of the contract. Then they left, but not before giving Sabrina her schoolbooks.

"Great," Sabrina groaned. "I'm engaged to a troll *and* I have to study for finals."

Standing by the door through which her aunts had left, Sabrina said, "If they're not back by Friday, I'll flunk biology."

"Forget about homework!" Roland blurted. "You're my princess now, like in a fairy tale!"

That said, Roland waved his hand and Sabrina's clothes were instantly transformed. Sabrina was now dressed in a flowing pink gown with a tall, pointy hat. She groaned. "I can dress *myself*, thank you very much!" she said.

When Hilda and Zelda returned, Mr. Clarkson announced that he had found a hidden clause in the troll's contract: Sabrina could be rescued by a prince she desired!

"A prince?" Hilda muttered.

"Where are we going to find a prince Sabrina desires?" asked Zelda.

Just then the doorbell rang. It was Harvey. When Zelda told him Sabrina wasn't home, he turned to leave. Then she caught sight of "THE TERMITE KING" printed on the back of his jacket.

"Who is the 'Termite King'?" Zelda asked.

"My dad," said Harvey. "That's his business."

"Which makes you the Termite *Prince*!" exclaimed Zelda.

Mr. Clarkson studied his law book for a moment, then said Harvey would do.

The aunts were excited! But Harvey could not learn the truth about Sabrina, so they whipped up a memory-loss potion. Then they explained everything to Harvey, and told him that once he'd rescued Sabrina, the potion would remove it all from his memory.

Back in the castle, Roland was talking with Camilla, the wedding coordinator. As Roland and Camilla laughed cheerfully together, Sabrina said, "I've got an idea. Why don't *you* two get married?"

"Poor Sabrina," Roland said. "Maybe I shouldn't put you through this stress."

"*Really?*" Sabrina gasped hopefully. "You mean . . . ?"

"Yes!" Roland cried. "Let's have the wedding *tomorrow!*"

Meanwhile the aunts led Harvey up to the linen closet. Just as he was about to enter it, Hilda said, "Wait. Your clothes are all wrong." She magically dressed him in a prince's outfit, complete with tights and a sword. Then they pushed him into the closet and closed the door.

Harvey found himself outside Roland's castle. He tried the door, but it wouldn't open. He looked up at a window in the castle's turret and shouted, "Sabrina!"

"Harvey!" Sabrina exclaimed, leaning out the window. "What are *you* doing here?"

"I'm supposed to vanquish the troll," he said. "But the door is locked."

There had to be a way to get Harvey into the castle.

"Think fairy tales," Sabrina said to herself. Finally, she had an idea. "I've got it!" she cried.

Sabrina pointed at her hair. It grew so long that it gathered at her feet in a shimmering golden pool. She threw all her hair out the window and told Harvey to start climbing up the long strands.

Harvey struggled up Sabrina's long tresses and crawled clumsily through the window. *Thunk!* He landed on the floor. Sabrina rushed to help Harvey to his feet. She gave him a big hug and exclaimed, "My prince has come!"

"Yeah, but these tights are bunching up on me," Harvey said.

Holding Harvey's hands, Sabrina said, "I'm so glad you're here."

"Me too," said Harvey, as he looked around the room. "But how are we ever going to get out of this castle without getting caught by that little guy?"

Suddenly Roland burst into the room with his sword drawn!

"You will *not* leave this realm alive, Farm Boy!" Roland growled.

"I hate it when you call me that!" Harvey snapped. With great effort, he drew his sword. Their blades clashed. Roland backed Harvey out the door and down the stairs. Sabrina ran to the window.

She tried to help Harvey by shouting things like, "To
your left! Watch out! *Duck*!" But it was no use. Harvey was
no match for Roland's sword-fighting skills.

Finally, Roland knocked the sword from Harvey's hand.
With one foot on Harvey's chest, he said triumphantly,
"You've drawn your last breath, Farm Boy."

It was not over yet!

Sabrina grabbed her schoolbooks.

"Don't worry!" she called. "Here comes the air support!"

Holding her biggest, thickest book out the window, she quickly cast a spell. "My aim is true," she said.

The book landed right on Roland's head! The troll dropped to the ground. Sabrina raced down the stairs and hugged Harvey.

"What happened?" Roland asked, rubbing his head. "Sabrina, did *you* do this to me?"

"Consider yourself vanquished," Sabrina said. Then she took Harvey's hand and they headed for home.

A while later, the memory-loss potion took effect. Harvey was studying for the biology finals with Sabrina. He had no memory of their adventure—or of Sabrina's secret—but Sabrina would never forget the day her handsome prince came to her rescue!

# SWEEPSTAKES

## What would you do with Sabrina's magic powers?

You could win a visit to the set,
a $1000 savings bond, and
other magical prizes!

**GRAND PRIZE:** A tour of the set of *Sabrina, The Teenage Witch* and a savings bond worth $1000 upon maturity

**10 FIRST PRIZES:** Sabrina's Cauldron, filled with one Sabrina, The Teenage Witch CD-ROM, one set of eight Archway Paperbacks, one set of three Simon Spotlight children's books, and one Hasbro Sabrina fashion doll

**25 SECOND PRIZES:** One Sabrina, The Teenage Witch CD-ROM

**50 THIRD PRIZES:** One Hasbro Sabrina fashion doll

**100 FOURTH PRIZES:** A one-year subscription to Sabrina, The Teenage Witch comic book, published by Archie Comics

# Sabrina, The Teenage Witch™ Sweepstakes Official Rules:

1. No Purchase Necessary. Enter by mailing the completed Official Entry Form or by mailing on a 3" x 5" card your name, address, and daytime telephone number to Pocket Books/Sabrina, The Teenage Witch Sweepstakes, 13th Floor, 1230 Avenue of the Americas, NY, NY 10020. Entries must be received by 7/1/98. Not responsible for lost, late, damaged, stolen, illegible, mutilated, incomplete, not delivered entries, or for typographical errors in the entry form or rules. Entries are void if they are in whole or in part illegible, incomplete, or damaged. Enter as often as you wish, but each entry must be mailed separately. Winners will be selected at random from all eligible entries received in a drawing to be held on or about 7/7/98. Winners will be notified by mail.

2. Prizes: One Grand Prize: A weekend (four days/three nights) trip to Los Angeles for two people including round-trip coach airfare from the major airport nearest the winner's residence, ground transportation or car rental, meals, three nights in a hotel (one room, occupancy for two), and a tour of the set of Sabrina, The Teenage Witch (approximate retail value $3500.00) and a savings bond worth $1000 ($US) upon maturity in 18 years. Travel accommodations are subject to availability; certain restrictions apply. 10 First Prizes: Sabrina's Cauldron, filled with one CD-ROM (a Windows 95 compatible program), one set of eight Sabrina, The Teenage Witch books published by Archway Paperbacks, one set of three Simon Spotlight children's books, and one Hasbro Sabrina fashion doll (approximate retail value $100). 25 Second Prizes: Sabrina, The Teenage Witch CD-ROM, published by Simon & Schuster Interactive (approximate retail value $30). 50 Third Prizes: Sabrina, The Teenage Witch doll (approximate retail value $17.99). 100 Fourth Prizes: a one-year subscription to Sabrina, The Teenage Witch comic book, published by Archie Comics (approximate retail value $15). The Grand Prize must be taken on the dates specified by sponsors.

3. The sweepstakes is open to legal residents of the U.S. and Canada (excluding Quebec). Prizes will be awarded to the winner's parent or legal guardian if under 18. Any minor taking a Grand Prize trip must be accompanied by a parent or legal guardian. Void in Puerto Rico and wherever prohibited or restricted by law. All federal, state, and local laws apply. Employees of Viacom International, Inc., their families living in the same household, and its subsidiaries and their affiliates and their respective agencies and participating retailers are not eligible.

4. One prize per person or household. Prizes are not transferabl and may not be substituted except by sponsors, in event of prize unavailability, in which case a prize of equal or greater value will be awarded. All prizes will be awarded. The odds of winning a prize depend upon the number of eligible entries received.

5. If a winner is a Canadian resident, then he/she must correctly answer a skill-based question administered by mail.

6. All expenses on receipt and use of prize, including federal, state and local taxes, are the sole responsibility of the winners. Winner may be required to execute and return an Affidavit of Eligibility and Release and all other legal documents that the sweepstakes sponso may require (including a W-9 tax form) within 15 days of attempte notification or an alternate winner will be selected. Grand Prize Winner's travel companion will be required to execute a liabilit release prior to ticketing.

7. By accepting a prize, winners or winners' parents or lego guardians on winners' behalf agree to allow use of their names photographs, likenesses, and entries for any advertising, promotion and publicity purposes without further compensation to o permission from the entrants, except where prohibited by law.

8. By participating in this sweepstakes, entrants agree to be bound by these rules and the decisions of the judges and sweepstake sponsors, which are final in all matters relating to the sweepstakes.

9. For a list of major prizewinners (available after 7/15/98), send a stamped, self-addressed envelope to Prizewinners, Pocke Books/Sabrina, The Teenage Witch Sweepstakes, 13th Floor, 1230 Avenue of the Americas, NY, NY 10020.

10. Simon & Schuster is the official sweepstakes sponsor.

11. The sweepstakes sponsors shall have no liability for any injury loss, or damage of any kind arising out of participation in this sweepstakes or the acceptance or use of the prize. Viacom Productions, Paramount Pictures, and Archie Comic Publications, Inc. and their respective parent and affiliated companies are no responsible for fulfillment of prizes or for any loss, damage, or injury suffered as a result of the set tour or use or acceptance of prizes.

## Official Entry Form

Name _____

Address _____

City _____ State _____ Zip _____

Phone _____